**Gazelle Books** are a series of lively and enjoyable stories which are ideal for children who have just started to read by themselves. Each story, with its clear, large type, is simple but complete and will be invaluable in helping children to move from picture books to first story books. Written by first-class authors and packed with illustrations, Gazelle Books are fun to read!

*About the author*

**Sheila Lavelle** lives in Kirkcudbright, Scotland. She has always enjoyed writing for children and Hamish Hamilton have been publishing her books for fifteen years. Sheila has written several stories about Ursula for both the Gazelle and Cartwheels series, and she is also the creator of the 'Fiend' books for older readers. Sheila is married with two children, and has two border collies.

GAZELLE

# URSULA BALLOONING

*by*

## SHEILA LAVELLE

*Illustrated by*
*Thelma Lambert*

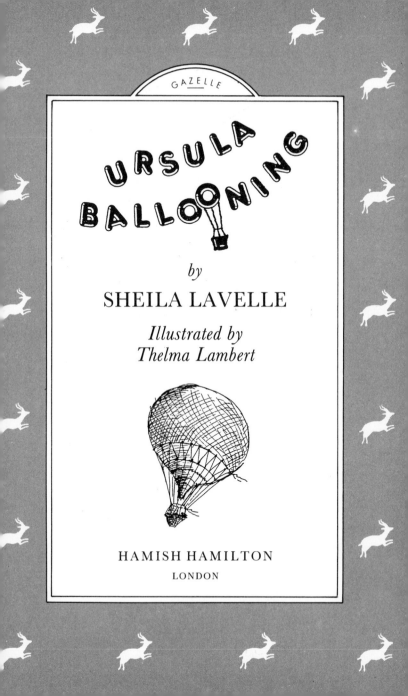

HAMISH HAMILTON

LONDON

## HAMISH HAMILTON LTD

Published by the Penguin Group
27 Wrights Lane, London w8 5tz, England
Penguin Books USA Inc., 375 Hudson Street, New York,
New York 10014, USA
Penguin Books Australia Ltd, Ringwood, Victoria, Australia
Penguin Books Canada Ltd, 10 Alcorn Avenue, Toronto, Ontario,
Canada m4v 3b2
Penguin Books (NZ) Ltd, 182–190 Wairau Road, Auckland 10, New Zealand

Penguin Books Ltd, Registered Offices: Harmondsworth, Middlesex, England

First published in Great Britain 1992 by Hamish Hamilton Ltd

British Library Cataloguing in Publication Data
CIP data for this book is available from the British Library

ISBN 0-241-13202-9

Set in 15pt Baskerville by Rowland Phototypesetting Ltd
Bury St Edmunds, Suffolk
Printed in Great Britain by BPCC Hazells Ltd
Member of BPCC Ltd

## Chapter One

Ursula and Fredbear came home
from school one Friday afternoon to
find Aunt Prudence watching the
local news on television.

"Look, Ursula," said Aunt
Prudence. "Hot-air balloons. Aren't
they lovely?"

Ursula gave a gasp of wonder.
Floating in the sky, above a hillside
dotted with trees, were a dozen
enormous balloons. Striped and
patterned in all colours of the

rainbow, they glowed like lamps in the sky. It was one of the most beautiful sights Ursula had ever seen.

"Wow!" she breathed. "I wish I could have a ride in one of those. Don't you, Fredbear?"

Fredbear had fallen upside-down in a corner of the sofa and wouldn't even look.

"They're talking about flights at Hill Green," said Aunt Prudence. Ursula sat down to listen.

"Tickets are available from Barton travel agents," the news-reader was saying. "Trips start at ten o'clock tomorrow morning at Hill Green. Landings will be in Plunton Park, if the present wind speed and

direction continues . . ."

Ursula bounced on the sofa in excitement. "He said tomorrow morning! At Hill Green! Can we go, Aunt Prudence? Please?"

Aunt Prudence laughed.

"Don't be silly, Ursula," she said, getting up to put the kettle on. "Hot-air balloon flights cost pots of money."

"I've got pots of money," said Ursula. "Gran sent me some for my birthday last week."

She jumped up from the sofa and ran upstairs to raid her piggybank.

Ursula hurried along the High Street a little while later, with Fredbear in her arms and a purse stuffed with

4

money in her pocket.

She had taken every single penny
out of her piggybank, and what a lot
of money it was, even if you didn't
count the Spanish peseta and the
buttons from her old pink dress.

Ursula didn't know exactly how much she had. But she was sure it was enough for a hot-air balloon flight, in spite of what Aunt Prudence had said. Find out for yourself, her aunt had told her, and that was just what Ursula intended to do.

Ursula pushed open the glass door of the Travel Agency. She ignored the brochures about villas in Portugal and skiing in Switzerland and hang-gliding in Timbuctoo, and went straight up to the desk.

"I want a ride in a hot-air balloon, please," she said importantly. She opened her purse and tipped the money out on the counter.

A pale young man with spiky hair

like a hedgehog looked at Ursula in astonishment.

"A hot-air balloon?" he said, as if he had never heard of such a thing. Two girls with dangling earrings and purple lips as if they had been eating blackberries turned from their computers to stare at Ursula.

"Yes, a ticket for a pleasure flight," said Ursula. "At Hill Green tomorrow. I saw it on the telly."

The man scratched his head and made his hair spikier than ever. The two girls looked at one another and giggled.

The man poked Ursula's money about with his finger. Then he shook his head.

"Not enough," he said. "Hot-air ballooning is expensive. It's for grown-ups with plenty of money, not for little girls like you."

Ursula stood on tiptoe to make herself taller. "How much is it, then, for a ride in a hot-air balloon?"

The man pointed to a poster on the wall.

"HOT-AIR BALLOON FLIGHTS," the poster said. "SATURDAY 1ST JUNE FROM HILL GREEN. WEATHER PERMITTING. TICKETS £100."

Ursula's mouth fell open.

"A hundred pounds!" she gasped. "Good grief!"

She grabbed the money and stuffed it back in her purse.

"Come on, Fredbear," she said. "It's daylight robbery."

And she marched indignantly out of the shop.

## Chapter Two

Ursula stomped along, not looking where she was going, and walked straight into a lady in a green dress that almost reached the ground.

"Ursula!" said a voice. "What ebber is the matter? You look down in the dump."

It was Mrs Martinez, who was Spanish and had trouble with the letter 'v'. She painted pictures and played the flute, and she lived in a house full of cobwebs where it didn't

matter if you dropped crisp crumbs
on the floor.

"Come and hab an ice-cream,"
said Mrs Martinez. "You can tell me
all about it."

Ursula felt better sitting in the
park licking a strawberry ice-cream.
She sat on a bench in the sunshine
and told Mrs Martinez the whole
story. Mrs Martinez listened right to

the end without butting in once, and
Fredbear sat between them and
didn't interrupt either.

"Good hebbens. A hundred
pounds!" said Mrs Martinez, when
Ursula had finished. "It's daylight
robbery!"

"That's what I said," said Ursula,
licking ice-cream off her wrist.

Mrs Martinez looked thoughtful.

"Where are these balloon flights?" she asked. "Hill Green, you say?"

"They start at Hill Green at ten," said Ursula. "They'll come down in Plunton Park, if the wind stays the same as it is now."

"So they should be flying over Four Oaks about lunch-time," said Mrs Martinez. "Why don't we go and watch them? I'll bring a picnic, and we should get a good biew from there, no?"

"A good what?" said Ursula. "Oh, a good view!"

Ursula knew that watching the balloons going over Four Oaks Hill wouldn't be half as good as riding in one, but it was better than nothing.

14

She tucked Fredbear under her arm and stood up.

"Thank you, Mrs Martinez," she said. "That'll be great."

Mrs Martinez beamed. "I'll pick you up at twelve o'clock. What shall I bring for the picnic?"

"A currant bun, please," said Ursula, turning to run off home. "You never know when it might come in useful."

## Chapter Three

There was a very good reason why
Ursula had asked Mrs Martinez to
bring a currant bun. A currant bun,
filled with a special magic mixture of
porridge oats and honey, was all
Ursula needed to turn herself into a
bear.

Ursula had found the spell in the
library, and to her astonishment it
really worked. She could turn herself
into a real, live bear whenever she
liked, and a beefburger and chips

were all she needed to turn back into a girl again.

Aunts are sometimes not very keen on people turning into bears, so Ursula kept it a secret from Aunt Prudence. But Mrs Martinez knew all about it, and it didn't bother her a bit.

Mrs Martinez stopped the car outside Ursula's front door at twelve o'clock the next day and tooted the horn.

Ursula kissed Aunt Prudence goodbye. Then she picked up Fredbear and ran out to the car.

"All right, Ursula?" said Mrs Martinez, smiling in her best yellow T-shirt. "The wind is the same as yesterday, yes?"

"Yes, I heard it on the radio," said Ursula happily. "I can't wait to see the balloons." She turned to wave at Aunt Prudence on the doorstep, then she settled Fredbear in her lap and sat back to enjoy the ride.

Half an hour later Ursula was not feeling quite so happy. It was beginning to look as if the whole world had come to watch the balloons.

"What a crowd!" said Ursula in dismay as they drove up Four Oaks Hill towards the clump of trees at the top.

"We won't see a thing," said
Ursula crossly, as she unpacked the
sandwiches and the currant bun with
the special magic filling of porridge
oats and honey. "All I can see is
legs."

Hundreds of cars were parked in rows on the hillside. People with cameras and binoculars pushed and jostled for the best views towards Hill Green. There was even a television film crew, with a fat man in an orange vest shouting and bossing everybody about.

Mrs Martinez found a space to park the car under the trees at the very top of the hill. Then she and Ursula had to push their way through the crowd before they could spread the rug out on the grass.

Suddenly a shout went up from somebody at the front.

"Here come the balloons!"

Mrs Martinez turned to look at the four tall oak trees behind them. "It's a pity you can't climb a tree," she said to Ursula. "You'd get the best view of all from up there."

Ursula stared at Mrs Martinez.

Why hadn't she thought of it before?

"I'm not very good at climbing trees, Mrs Martinez," she said. "But I know somebody who is!"

She picked up the currant bun and began to munch it down.

"I'M A BEAR, I'M A BEAR, I'M A BEAR," she mumbled, trying not to spit crumbs out at Mrs Martinez.

"I'M A BEAR, I'M A BEAR, I'M A BEAR."

Everybody was busy watching the balloons. Nobody noticed when Ursula suddenly vanished and a small brown bear appeared in her place. Nobody except Mrs Martinez and Fredbear, that is, and they had seen it all before.

"Good luck, Ursula Bear," said Mrs Martinez, as Ursula scampered gleefully off towards the nearest tree.

## Chapter Four

Bears are excellent climbers, and it took Ursula no more than a minute to reach the top of the tree. She crawled out to the end of the highest branch and looked down for the first time.

The ground was a very long way down, and Mrs Martinez had been right. The view from up here was amazing.

"Coo-ee! Mrs Martinez!" called Ursula in her growly bear's voice, spotting the yellow T-shirt far below and waving her paw. But Mrs Martinez didn't see her. She was too busy watching the sky like everybody else.

Ursula leaned forward, searching the ground for Fredbear. Then a sudden strange hissing, roaring sound made her look up instead of down.

"Crumbs!" she said, almost falling out of the tree in astonishment, for floating towards her was the first of the hot-air balloons.

Ursula gulped when she saw how huge and how close it was. It was so close that she could feel the heat from the roaring gas burner. She could see the passengers in the basket, a man with a ginger moustache and two ladies, one fat and one thin. They were all wearing crash helmets, and they were all gazing at the trees in alarm.

"Look out!" the man shouted. "We're going to hit those trees!"

"Help!" growled Ursula, trying to scramble out of the way.

She was too late. There was a loud splintering crash as the heavy basket collided with Ursula's branch. The force of the crash knocked Ursula clean off her perch and sent her tumbling head over heels into the basket.

The basket rocked wildly, then freed itself. It finally went sailing safely on, full of leaves and twigs.

26

Ursula scrambled out from under
the leaves. She shook the twigs out of
her fur and peered over the edge of
the basket.

"Wow!" she growled. "I'm in a
balloon! Isn't it great!"

27

The other passengers had gone as pale as porridge and were gaping at Ursula with their mouths open. The man with the ginger moustache had his leg over the side of the basket as if he were going to jump out.

"Help, a bear!" he cried. "It's going to bite me!"

The thin lady grabbed his arm to stop him from falling, and they both pressed backwards into a corner as far away from Ursula as possible. Ursula couldn't talk except in bear language, and growling only made things worse, so she held out her paws to show that she meant no harm.

It was the fat lady who pulled herself together first.

"I er . . . think it's all right," she gulped. "It's only a small cub. And it seems to be quite tame."

Ursula nodded her head as hard as she could and offered the fat lady a twig as a present.

"There, did you see that?" said the fat lady. "It must be somebody's pet."

"I don't care what it is," said the man with the ginger moustache. "Just keep it away from me, that's all."

He stood up and looked over the side. "Give this thing a bit more gas, Janet," he said hastily. "Or we'll all end up in the river."

The burner roared. The hot air inside the balloon got hotter and hotter. Up and up into the sky rose the basket, with Ursula in it.

Ursula held her breath as she watched the earth getting farther and farther away. If only Mrs Martinez and Fredbear could see her now!

## Chapter Five

Ursula was enjoying the flight so much that at first she didn't think about where the balloon was taking her. But after a while, as they sailed on over fields and rivers and churches and villages, she began to worry. Riding in a balloon was great fun, but how was she going to get back home? How was she going to turn back into a girl again? And what was Mrs Martinez doing all this time?

Although Ursula didn't know it, Mrs Martinez had seen everything that had happened. And she had wasted no time in grabbing Fredbear and the picnic and dashing back to the car. Now she was following Ursula as fast as the old car would go, praying that the balloon wouldn't sail away out of sight.

Ursula felt sorry when the balloon began to descend and her wonderful adventure was over, but she was very relieved all the same when she looked over the side and saw Mrs Martinez' car following close behind.

As the balloon started to come down into a meadow, Mrs Martinez turned off the bumpy road and drove through a gate. She parked the car

beside the hedge and jumped out.

The balloon was only a few metres from the ground when Mrs Martinez ran out across the grass. A cow stopped chewing and stared in surprise.

"Ursula!" shouted Mrs Martinez, waving both arms. "Coo-ee!"

"Grrrrrr!" Ursula called back, leaning out and waving both paws.

"There's somebody down there waving," said the fat lady. "And the bear seems to know her!"

"Well, whoever it is had better get out of the way," said the man. "Or we'll be landing on her head."

The basket thumped on the ground, once, twice, and then stayed still. The passengers were so busy untangling ropes and pegging the balloon down before it blew away that they forgot all about the bear.

Ursula scrambled out of the basket and scampered across the field.

"Grr!" she said, hugging Mrs Martinez with both paws. "Gr-gr-grrrrrrr!"

"I didn't understand a word of that," said Mrs Martinez. "But I expect it means beefburger and cheeps, yes?"

Ursula turned three cartwheels on the grass before jumping into the car.

## Chapter Six

Ursula and Fredbear waited outside
the Burger Bar. While they waited
they amused themselves by making
faces through the car window at the
astonished passers-by, including the
pale young man from the travel
agency, who almost fell over in
surprise.

Mrs Martinez soon came back
with a warm paper parcel.

"Do your magic, Ursula," she said.
"And let's get you safely home."

"RAEB A M'I, RAEB A M'I, RAEB A M'I," growled Ursula, gobbling beefburger and chips with salt and vinegar and tomato ketchup. "RAEB A M'I, RAEB A M'I, RAEB A M'I!"

By the time Mrs Martinez drew up outside Aunt Prudence's front door, the little bear had disappeared. Ursula was quite herself again, and

none the worse for her adventure, except for a smear of tomato ketchup on her chin.

"There you are!" said Aunt Prudence, opening the door to let them in. "Did you have a nice time, Ursula? I suppose you're going to tell me you had a ride in a hot-air balloon?"

Ursula didn't know what to say. She didn't want to tell a lie, so she couldn't say yes or no.

She thought for a moment. "It was very expensive," she said at last. "The tickets cost a hundred pounds."

Aunt Prudence put the kettle on for tea.

"A hundred pounds!" she snorted.

"It's daylight robbery!"

Ursula and Mrs Martinez grinned at one another.

"That's just what we said!" they laughed together.

And off went Ursula to put Fredbear to bed. He was looking quite worn out after all the excitement.